DECIDE & SURVIVE ™

THE DESTRUCTION OF POMPEII

Published by Milk & Cookies, an imprint of Bushel & Peck Books. Bushel & Peck Books
is a family-run publishing house in Fresno, California, that believes in uplifting children
with the highest standards of art, music, literature, and ideas. Find beautiful books for
gifted young minds at www.bushelandpeckbooks.com.

Type set in LTC Kennerley Pro and Bobby Jones.
Graphic elements licensed from Shutterstock.com.

Bushel & Peck Books is dedicated to fighting illiteracy all over the world.
For every book we sell, we donate one to a child in need—book for book.
To nominate a school or an organization to receive free books,
please visit www.bushelandpeckbooks.com.

LCCN: TK
ISBN: 978-1-63819-180-3

First Edition

Printed in the United States

1 3 5 7 9 10 8 6 4 2

CAN YOU CHANGE POMPEII'S FATE?

SYLVIA WHITMAN | MIKE ANDERSON

MILK +
COOKIES

YOUR CALL TO ADVENTURE!

Dear Reader, this is *your* story. *You* control how history happens through the choices you make.

Don't read this book from the first page to the last. Instead, follow the directions at the bottom of each page. When you're offered options, choose wisely because your decision could end in disaster as easily as triumph.

No matter how your story ends, feel free to start over and create a different story with a new outcome.

Adventure, mystery, danger, and fortune await. Good luck!

BACKSTORY

It's 79 CE (common era), and the Roman Empire rules a quarter of the world's population. Rome has grown from a small Italian city into the capital of a vast realm that extends from England to North Africa and the Middle East.

You live in Rome's vacation playground, the balmy southern region known as Campania. Markets brim with nature's bounty: fish and meat, fruits and nuts. Cargo ships carry wares across the Mediterranean Sea. For the powerful and well-to-do, Campania is a paradise.

Except for the ticking time bomb at its heart.

A volcano.

Scenic Mount Vesuvius last erupted about 800 years ago. Everyone has forgotten that it can blow its top. Sheep graze and grapes grow on its fertile slopes. Rich Romans relax in grand villas in the towns below, which form a semicircle around the Bay of Naples.

Earthquakes regularly rattle this stretch of the Italian peninsula. Yet no one has a clue that superhot magma is seething below the surface.

Including you, 11-year-old Quintus.

You have no last name because you're a slave.

The Roman Empire depends on slaves. They build

aqueducts to move water. They mine metals to make weapons and coins. They battle each other in arenas to entertain crowds.

Some slaves work on farms, some in factories, some in religious temples or government offices. Many slaves, like you, work as household servants.

You serve a top Roman official, Gaius Plinius Secundus, known as Pliny the Elder. He's been a soldier, a lawyer, and a government official all over the empire. Three years ago, the emperor put him in charge of the naval base at Misenum, on the Bay of Naples.

Pliny the Elder commands about 50 warships and 10,000 men.

Really, he'd rather write books. That's why he had you educated, so you could help.

As a slave, you have no rights. You are a piece of property. You can be sold, rented, beaten, or killed. If you run away, a slavecatcher might hunt you down. Your owner might have you branded on the forehead with a hot iron.

On the other hand, a number of Romans free their slaves. These freedmen become citizens.

You want freedom. Dignity. A full name. A good life.

How can you pursue this dream beside a volcano about to explode?

➲ **BEGIN YOUR ADVENTURE ON THE NEXT PAGE.**

YOUR ADVENTURE BEGINS

"Where was I, Quintus?" Pliny the Elder demands from his bath.

You glance at the words you've inked onto papyrus.

"You were describing the orca, Sir. The huge whale that eats other whales."

"Ah, yes." Pliny waves to a slave to ready his towel and slippers. "An enormous mass of flesh armed with teeth."

Pliny stands, dripping and naked, his huge belly as white as the marble floor. *Speaking of an enormous mass of flesh armed with teeth . . .*

You feel a giggle rising.

Then the room trembles, sloshing the bathwater. You cork the giggle.

"How many of these quakes since midnight, Quin-tus?"

"Two, Sir."

"Note that."

Pliny may wheeze like an aging whale, but his mind is impressive. He's curious about everything. If he's not reading, he's writing. During meals, on the road, right up until bed—he's always working on his ency-clopedia, *Natural History*.

He hardly sleeps. His day—and yours—starts hours before dawn.

After 37 volumes, Pliny says that he's done. Almost. Something new always grabs his attention.

Pliny sends you to fetch his breakfast. Maybe you can help yourself to something along the way.

➲ **TO DETOUR FOR A NAP, GO TO PAGE 34.**

➲ **TO SEEK A SERVING OF FAMILY HISTORY, GO TO PAGE 45.**

Your opinion doesn't matter. You're a slave. Pliny will do exactly as he pleases.

"Rome, Sir," you say.

Vacation! Not really, of course. You don't get vacations. Or days off. But at least if you travel to Rome, you'll have a break from Pliny's endless demands.

Downside: You'll have to travel with Whiny.

Upside 2: In Rome, you can prove yourself. Observe. Take notes. Maybe one day, Pliny will think so highly of you that he'll grant your freedom.

Bonus 1: You might even catch a glimpse of Emperor Titus.

Bonus 2: Maybe you can find out more about your parents.

So, you set out with Whiny and his mother. They sit inside the large wagon on comfy silk cushions, under the wooden cover, along with Plinia's personal slaves.

You ride outside next to the driver, behind the mules.

Not long after you've left Misenum, the ground shudders. Plinia screams, and the mules stop cold. The underground winds must be gusting. Either that or some giant is throwing a temper tantrum.

The driver clucks his tongue, but the mules refuse to budge. He whips them until they step forward.

Mules are the slaves of slaves.

Their hooves strike a steady beat on the huge paving stones. *Clop, clop, clop, clop, pfft.* Mules fart just as much as horses.

You're on the Appian Way, queen of roads, when Vesuvius erupts with a thud. At this safe distance, you survive!

You can look forward to a lifetime as Whiny's slave.

THE END

"One more thing," Pliny says. "After you've gathered information, I want you to report it to the surgeon in Herculaneum."

Herculaneum? The ritzy small town north of Pompeii?

"You question my orders with your face, Quintus."

"Never, Sir. It's just . . . you will find many more different people, more different ideas, in Pompeii. Because of the seaport and the river coming together."

"You reason well." But Pliny says no more.

Before you leave, he hands you two letters. One is an open piece of papyrus identifying you as the admiral's slave. The other is a small roll, sealed with wax and stamped with Pliny's signet ring.

It's addressed to the surgeon G. Plinius G.L. Felix.

The *L* stands for *liberatus*, a freed slave. Freedmen's names usually reference the previous owner. G. Plinius—G as in Gaius? Did the surgeon used to belong to Pliny?

You have no time to ponder this. The majordomo sweeps you and a handful of other house slaves toward the ship.

You bend down, pretending to dislodge a stone in your sandal. Instead, you pick up a black rock and drop it into the leather pouch slung over your shoulder.

You board. Within minutes, the crew pushes away from the dock. Oars hover above the water. The piper toots. As one, the marines lower their blades into the water. They pull as the piper sets the pace, each note a stroke, perfectly in sync.

You love being on the water, tickled by spray from below, shadowed by birds above. Your hand rests in your pouch. Your fingers feel its contents: tablets, stylus, chestnuts picked off Pliny's tray.

Letters.

Rock. Just in case you decide to break the seal.

➲ **TO OPEN THE SEALED LETTER, GO TO PAGE 102.**

➲ **TO RESIST THAT TEMPTATION, GO TO PAGE 38.**

You kick Victor to move toward the white blobs. In several places, the earth has sunk.

Your head aches. Victor is panting. Why are you here on this mountain? Victor stumbles. You call him Spurius. You feel seasick. Or horsesick.

You're right at the edge of the mysterious pile when you realize they're sheep.

Dead sheep.

That's your last thought before you succumb to carbon dioxide poisoning.

THE END

It's only a four-hour walk to Herculaneum. But in the heat, you're flagging. Too bad you're not Hercules. Then you'd run. Everyone would throw flowers at you, the hometown demigod.

Sea breezes greet you. Herculaneum is lovely, with villas overlooking the sea. Pine trees and mulberries rise behind walls draped with flowering vines.

You ask around and find a small house with a sign: G. Plinius G.L. Felix, surgeon. Next to the name are pictures for people who can't read: a doctor setting a broken leg, cutting out a tumor, bandaging a wound. In one image, a woman catches a baby.

You lift the door knocker and tap three times.

➲ **CONTINUE TO PAGE 92.**

The rocky missiles are giving you a pounding headache. "We need better helmets," you say.

Five seconds later, you and Spurius both shout: "Like gladiators!"

Dodging falling bricks, you trudge with Ferox to the gladiators' barracks.

It's a wreck—columns down, roof collapsed in the corner. You clamber over rubble into one of the rooms.

Such cool weapons—tridents, daggers, spears, knives, maces, swords. You and Spurius each grab a gladius and square off. You recite the gladiator pledge together: "I will endure to be burned, to be bound, to be beaten, and to be killed by the sword."

Ferox whines, so you both look around. In the doorway glowers a muscled warrior holding a curved sword. You recognize him and his sica from posters. And from graffiti: *Celadus, the Thracian, who makes the girls' hearts beat faster.*

Your heart's beating faster for a different reason. Last month in the arena, Celadus used his sica to carve up his opponent.

"What are you doing?" he thunders.

➜ **TO TAKE OFF, GO TO PAGE 20.**

➜ **TO EXPLAIN, GO TO PAGE 40.**

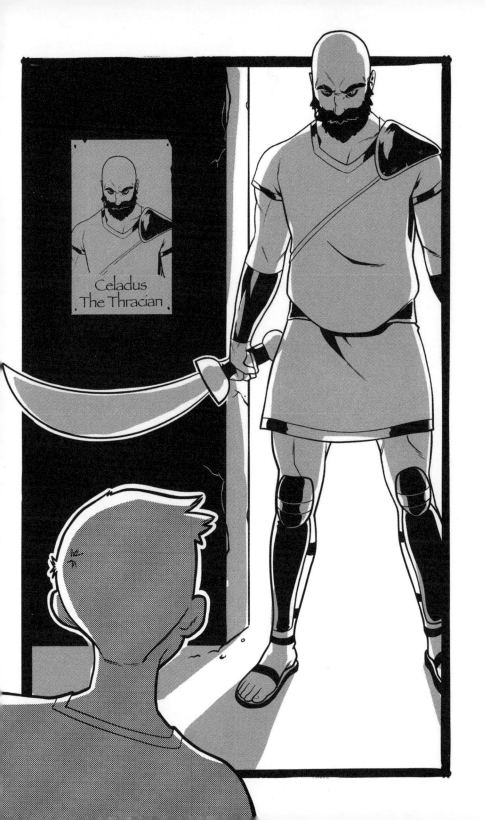

Celadus
The Thracian

"Run!" Spurius yells.

You drop your gladius and bolt out of the barracks, Ferox barking at your heels.

"To Venus," you say.

Back in the morass, past the Forum, down Via Marina. The Temple of Venus overlooks the sea. What's left of it anyway.

You and Spurius stand before the one statue remaining on its pedestal.

"Oh, great goddess of love," you start.

"Divine protector of Pompeii," Spurius continues.

"You're not doing a great job."

"Quintus!"

The ground shakes, and the marble goddess, all 600 pounds of her, flies down and flattens you.

Wrong place, wrong time.

THE END

You ask Spurius where to find a horse.

"You're in a stable, Blockhead!"

"I can't take one of these horses. Publius will kill me. And you."

"Only if he finds out," Spurius says. "He's going to the theater tonight. He'll be too drunk to notice."

You protest, but soon you are mounted on Victor, one of Pompeii's finest racehorses.

You set out at a walk. Once outside the city walls, you cluck your tongue. It's as if Victor can read your mind. Under a full moon, you thunder toward the black mountain looming over the countryside.

A trail twists up the mountainside. You relax the reins. Victor picks his way over ruts and rocks.

Suburban villas give way to farmhouses surrounded by fields and vineyards. Now and then a dog barks, but otherwise it's eerily quiet. No night birds hooting. No clear streams gurgling.

Almost with a groan, the ground stirs, a quake that seems to come from deep below. Victor freezes. You hang tightly to his neck. Will he bolt?

Minutes later—feels like hours—the shaking stops. These episodes are getting stronger, and longer. Danger lurks within the mountain. You're sure of it.

Pliny will demand evidence. He will ridicule your feeling.

On the other hand, he believes there are people with sixteen toes and backward feet.

➲ **TO CONTINUE EXPLORING MOUNT VESUVIUS, GO TO PAGE 57.**

➲ **TO TURN BACK, GO TO PAGE 23.**

Victor needs no prodding. He moves quickly down the trail. You're not going to Herculaneum, not now.

You muster facts for Pliny. Quakes. Silence. Heat. The soil on Mount Vesuvius is as black as cookfire coals. What if flame, not wind, lies beneath the ground?

You could embellish the truth. At the top of the mountain, you met a . . . giant, as tall as the Coliseum, with . . . sixteen rear ends, and every time he passes gas, the ground trembles. That covers both the giant and the wind angles.

You descend below the treeline. In the moonlight, you see . . . pillows?

➲ **TO INVESTIGATE, GO TO PAGE 16.**

➲ **TO CONTINUE TOWARD MISENUM, GO TO PAGE 109.**

You tell Pliny your fears.

He pooh-poohs you and sets off for Pompeii alone.

Whiny holes up in his room with his "homework." You straighten books in the library.

Meanwhile, the cloud widens, and the sky darkens.

You try to sleep, but the ground quakes as never before. Everyone gathers outside in the courtyard.

Morning dawns with the palest light. Whiny and his mother ride out in a chariot but return soon, unable to move forward with the rocking of the earth. The sea is roiling. Dead fish wash ashore. The cloud masks the far coast. Where Pliny is.

More fiery ash and rocks fall as the cloud creeps over land and sea.

Plinia begs Whiny to escape alone. Your respect for him goes up a notch when he insists they stick together. Your respect goes down two notches when Whiny and his mother abandon everyone else. Around you, servants wail. Townspeople pound at the gate, but the majordomo refuses them entry.

To your surprise, Whiny and his mother return again. They look shocked. They couldn't get far because of the crushing crowd. Men begged the gods for mercy—or cursed them. Women shrieked. Children sobbed.

And you didn't rescue any of them, Whiny?

After several days, a ship returns carrying Pliny's body. He died on the beach in Stabiae.

His will reveals his last wishes: He adopted Whiny and left him everything. Including you.

You serve Whiny over his long career as a lawyer, senator, and public official. He writes a lot—mostly letters. You have a laugh, though, when he gets appointed Rome's Curator of the City's Sewers.

THE END

"Will anybody notice if you're hard to find for an hour?"

"Publius went off in a litter to dinner," Spurius says. "Then he's going to the theater."

Together you head back along Via dell'Abbondanza. Usually water runs down the middle, washing out the sewage. Not today. Even the water fountains have dried up. Everything reeks.

Spurius stops in front of The Inn of the Mule-Drivers. "What does this say?"

You read him the graffiti scribbled on the wall: "We have pissed in our beds. Host, I admit that we shouldn't have done this. If you ask why? There was no potty."

Spurius cracks up. It's good to hear him laugh.

You look for other messages. Most concern the upcoming election, along the lines of "Vote for Claudius, an honest young man." You find one next to a house: "Whoever writes anything here let him rot and be nameless."

"We're already half nameless," says Spurius. "We should write something."

You pick up a chunk of charcoal. "What do you want to say?"

"Spurius the Great was here with his friend Quintus."

You write, then read aloud: "Spurius the Great was here with his friend Quintus the Greater."

Before Spurius can protest, the front door opens. A woman wearing a cloak steps out. When she spots you, her expression sours. Holy Juno! You and Spurius exchange one look and take off.

A tremor seizes the street. People scream. You and Spurius keep running, zigging and zagging around shoppers, dodging pots and flying tiles, racing past the Stabian Baths. Finally, the ground stills, and you lean over, panting and laughing.

"That was fun!" says Spurius.

⮕ TO TOOL AROUND POMPEII SOME MORE, GO TO PAGE 60.

⮕ TO HATCH A BOLD PLAN, GO TO PAGE 78.

Spurius insists you break into the iron lockboxes in the atrium. Publius has two, fixed on stone blocks, to show off how rich he is. Spurius knows exactly where the key is—on a chain in the porter's room.

"And he's just going to let us have it?"

"He won't know."

"Because . . . ?"

"He drank his first glass of wine before Publius even left."

The porter's not the only one drinking. Slaves shout over a dice game. You and Spurius hug the wall as you pass.

You hear snores from the porter's room. Spurius tiptoes in. Within a minute, he's back with the key.

Together you run to the atrium. You grab a torch off a bracket.

Spurius tries the key in the first lockbox.

Doesn't fit.

He curses, twisting the key left and right.

"Stop. You'll break it," you hiss.

Footsteps. Someone is walking down the corridor. Humming.

⮑ **CONTINUE TO PAGE 64.**

Germania, you and Spurius decide. Rome has fought long and hard to subdue tribes on the frontier. One side or the other will value your skills.

You'll head northeast, up the Adriatic coast. Your plan is like a colander—lots of holes, but with a shape.

"We need last names," you say.

"What about . . . Fortis?" Spurius says.

Quintus Fortis. The brave. Spurius Fortis. The strong.

"Fortis for both of us?"

"We're brothers," says Spurius.

That proves true for the rest of your long and adventurous lives.

THE END

"The river," Spurius says.

Heads down, you and Spurius trudge toward the Sarno.

Others have the same idea. People drop their belongings when they can no longer carry them, creating islands in this stream of ash. Bodies too. No one speaks. It's too terrible.

One step. Another. You imagine yourself a Roman legionnaire. You have trained for this, the long march. One step. Another.

At Ferox's sharp bark, you and Spurius look back. The dog is buried up to his chest. But Spurius turns around. Ferox is family.

Spurius tries cradling Ferox, but he's too heavy. You lift Ferox and lay him across Spurius's shoulders.

Vesuvius roars again. A molten flow barrels across the countryside, faster than any chariot Spurius would ever have driven.

It's a quick death.

THE END

You drag Spurius toward the spilled garum. You scoop up a handful of fermenting mackerel, tuna, and anchovies and smear it all over his tunic.

"What the—" Then he gets it. "So he can't smell me." He dips both hands into the goop and plasters your head and arms. "Or you."

Thoroughly mucked, you each grab an amphora and follow a longshoreman aboard. Once he's deposited his jug and goes back for another, you and Spurius hide among the giant terracotta containers.

Ferox's bark approaches, getting louder.

Then it fades . . . and finally disappears into the dockside hubbub.

The longshoremen wall you in with amphorae. "Foul smell," one of them says.

Ten days later, you emerge when the ship docks in the Roman colony of Carthage. People turn away from your funk.

You and Spurius use your last coins to splurge on a bath. There you hear of Pompeii's end.

"From the end spring new beginnings," Pliny wrote. You start your new life in North Africa.

THE END

You sleep with other slaves in a storage room. But that's the first place someone will look for you. So, you slip outside.

The courtyard is quieter than usual. Fountains that usually burble now trickle. Yesterday Pliny sent workmen to search for a leak in the town's pipes.

You flump down in a heap of mulch. A tangy breeze blows in from the bay. With any luck, you can snooze for a few . . .

Bzzz. Bzzz.

You flap your hand by your ear and drift off.

A bite. You slap your cheek. Got him.

Only he got you first.

Turns out that mosquito was carrying a deadly parasite. Soon fever and chills rack your body. You struggle to breathe. Your skin yellows. You bleed.

In about a week you die of malaria.

Bacteria and viruses lurk everywhere in the Roman Empire. If smallpox and tuberculosis don't get you, perhaps typhoid fever or lead poisoning will.

THE END

You promise Felix you'll catch up with them later. Maybe Pliny can figure out what's going on. And you owe him: He helped find your mother.

You also need to check on your friend Spurius.

An eerie darkness descends. Near the beach, people pile into boats, some of them so full they swamp.

You run along the beach. "Anybody need a captain? I work for the admiral of the fleet."

No need to go into detail. In the dark, no one can see that you're eleven.

Finally, a gruff voice answers, "Here."

A man holding a . . . club? . . . stands in a small cargo ship. You doubt he's the owner. But you need to get to Pompeii.

When you board, the man unties the rope. You direct him to row.

As soon as you raise the sail, he snarls, "I should have left you to rot."

Is he talking to you?

Suddenly, a dozen bodies rise from the deck like the dead from their graves. Pirates? Except pirates should know how to sail. Escaped slaves?

And they think you're a free man. Who might turn them in.

You bark orders. *Oars left.* How do you let them know you're an ally?

The wind is blowing southeast, in the direction of Pompeii. But so is ash. Hot, sharp rocks pound down from the sky. The men are cursing.

A rock strikes your cheek, drawing blood.

All along the shore, people scream for help.

Suddenly the man who hired you looms before your face. Instead of a club, he now holds a dagger.

"Get us out of here."

➲ **TO SAIL TOWARD MISENUM, GO TO PAGE 51.**

➲ **TO JUMP SHIP, GO TO PAGE 74.**

The ship reaches Pompeii before sunset. It's as if Neptune himself has been pushing from his watery kingdom. Or the oarsmen have been rowing extra hard because of the promise of a night on the town.

A strange smell wafts through the port. Pompeii always smells rank, a mix of pee and garum, the town's famous fishy condiment. But this malodor has new layers. A little rotten egg. A little burning sulfur. *Puteo!*

The majordomo wrinkles his nose. Then he sprinkles a few bronze pieces in your hand. You suspect he's kept most of the coins for himself. He tells you to return to the ship tomorrow morning.

You want to meet the mysterious surgeon in Herculaneum. But you need something to report. So, Pompeii first. Where to?

➲ **TO HEAD TO THE BASILICA, GO TO PAGE 49.**

➲ **TO SEEK OUT YOUR FRIEND SPURIOUS, GO TO PAGE 106.**

"Just trying to stay alive?" you croak. "Celadus. Sir."

You rack your brains for anything that might help you bond. If only Pliny were more into sports.

Celadus turns to leave.

"Wait, Sir. Maybe you have some thoughts?" You ignore Spurius's kick. "You've been in many life-and-death situations."

"What?" he scoffs. "You're going to find the weak spot of this . . . " He waves his hand toward the rain of destruction outside.

"Weak spot." You let the phrase hang. "It's underground."

"The amphitheater?" Spurius asks.

"It's not like Rome," says Celadus. "No underground tunnels."

"The aqueduct," you say.

You just need to get in.

Celadus leads you through the barracks. You suit up in metal shin guards, shoulder pads, and helmets with visors. Nothing fits Ferox.

Outside, the armor helps. But the debris strikes like a blacksmith's anvil. *Bing, bing, bing.*

You weave through dark streets to the Forum. You see few people, though you suspect many lay buried beneath the rubble. A woman holding a bundled baby leans out a second-story window. "Help!"

You move toward the door, but it's crushed.

Celadus positions himself. "I'll catch you. Baby first."

The woman hesitates but drops the bundle into Celadus's arms. He passes the baby to Spurius.

"Now jump."

The woman sobs.

You hear stones groan.

"Quintus!" Spurius screams. "Ferox! Get out of the—"

➲ **CONTINUE TO PAGE 52.**

"Eheu!"

"Gods above!"

You wake to exclamations. Your throat feels as if you've driven a team of horses over a dusty road. You're coated with . . . ash?

The ship is coasting since the oarsmen have stopped rowing. Everyone is looking toward Vesuvius.

A giant column of smoke rises through the air.

"The boy's an augur," the captain mutters.

He orders the crew back to stations. They row toward Misenum as if chased by a sea monster.

Are you an augur, able to interpret the signs of the gods? According to the majordomo, ash began falling at midday. An hour later, a cloud burst from the top of the mountain.

As soon as the liburnian docks, you dash up to Pliny's villa. The family is in the atrium. Pliny's dictating a description of the cloud. Plinia, meanwhile, is wringing her hands, begging him to stay.

"Quintus," Pliny says. "I smell that you disregarded my order about the bath."

You report what you observed.

"Sure you don't want to explore with me?" he asks Whiny.

"I have the homework you gave me this morning," Whiny says.

"What about you, Quintus?" Pliny asks.

⮕ **TO STICK WITH THE ADMIRAL, GO TO PAGE 58.**

⮕ **TO HANG BACK WITH PLINIA AND PLINY THE YOUNGER, GO TO PAGE 24.**

Think fast. You say, "Taking from the rich—"

"You thieves," the porter interrupts. "I'm going to lock you in those boxes. Let the master—"

"Taking from the rich to give to the poor." You hold out a pair of emerald earrings. "You can buy more than one glass of wine at Asellina's Tavern with these."

"Here dwells happiness," Spurius says.

The porter wavers. "Publius will know."

"He'll think the mistress lost her earrings at the baths."

He snatches them. You hustle to the stable.

➲ **GO TO PAGE 61.**

Aromas lure you toward the kitchen: garlic, rosemary, baking bread. Outside, roosters crow. Not long until sunrise.

Hunger gnaws your insides. Questions do too.

The cook is rinsing pig intestines for sausages. You decide to ask him. He's grouchy, but he likes gossip. And he's served Pliny a long time.

"Do you know anything about my parents?"

The cook stuffs ground lamb into the intestines. He cocks his head toward a pot by the fire. "You hungry?"

You spoon wheat porridge to the rim of a bowl.

"The master brought you home one day," the cook says.

"From where? Were my parents too poor to keep me? Was my father a prisoner of war?"

Suddenly the ground shakes. Pots and utensils clang like a musician's cymbala. You smell burning.

"Out of my way," yells the cook. "A curse on your questions!"

Interview over.

Maybe it's better that you don't know the whole sad story.

Still huffing, the cook hands you Pliny's tray. Beside hot bread he's arranged figs, cheese, chestnuts, black olives, and olive oil in a glass bowl. From a wide cup

rises the scent of watered-down wine simmered with herbs.

On the way back to the library, you place the tray on the floor and slide down beside it. What can you eat without Pliny noticing?

Quite a lot actually.

➲ **CONTINUE TO PAGE 62.**

Plinia screams. The pitcher falls on Whiny's skull with an appalling crack.

He collapses.

Dead?

A tiny part of you hopes so. Just because life is so unfair. How many slaves die for no good reason?

But a huge part of you hopes Whiny is only a little dinged. If he's dead, you might get blamed.

And Whiny has his moments. Once he gave you his old wooden sword to play with.

"Oooh," he moans.

Plinia begs her brother to summon a doctor.

Pliny isn't a big fan of the medical profession, though. "A physician is the only person who can kill another without a penalty," he says.

Well, a physician and a slave owner.

"Gaius will be fine," Pliny continues. "The new emperor's father and I had many more knocks on the head when we fought together in Germany."

Before Pliny can describe how he rose to commander of the cavalry, Plinia begs him to leave Misenum.

➲ **CONTINUE TO PAGE 68.**

It's a short walk from the Marina Gate to the Forum. Vendors sell their wares from carts in an open space surrounded by temples, baths, toilets, and public buildings with towering columns.

A group of men is talking on the Basilica steps. Most wear white tunics, finely woven. The man with pur‑ple stripes on his tunic must be a senator. A few have togas draped over them.

You move closer, catching a few words. "Money's in rebuilding. . . ." "He served flamingo tongue—to die for . . . tastes like ostrich. . . ." "My money's on the bear tonight in the arena. . . ." "They'll sell the gladiator's blood outside—they say it cures. . . . "

Pompeii still hasn't finished cleaning up from the big quake seventeen years ago. Homes collapse, and all these moneybags see is profit.

Nearby, a gravelly voice draws your attention. "All of them, dead."

You move closer. "What's dead?" you ask a man in line for oranges.

"His sheep. On the mountainside."

"My neighbor packed up his family," Gravel‑voice continues. "He's got a brother in Venetia."

"Seen any giants?" you call over the crowd.

"Giants? No."

"Streams have all run dry," another vendor says.

"Maybe the giants have drunk them all up," a customer says. Several people laugh.

"I've smelled Vulcan's smoke," a woman says.

"Are you sure it's not your—"

"Enough of that," growls an old man.

"Something's not right," mutters a young man selling wooden spoons. "If I had anywhere to go, I would."

You've heard enough.

➲ **TO RIDE TO MOUNT VESUVIUS, GO TO PAGE 70.**

➲ **TO HIKE TO HERCULANEUM, GO TO PAGE 17.**

"Where to?" you ask.

He slashes the air with his blade.

"Misenum it is." Surely Pliny has dispatched the imperial navy. With any luck, you'll meet the ships halfway.

You command the men to row HARD.

Not a bad idea, but Vesuvius has hurled so much debris into the sea that it's gummed up.

Stuck, stuck, stuck.

Out of luck, luck, luck.

Your unhappy customer stabs you.

He doesn't outlast you long, though. Wind casts an ember into the sail, which bursts into flames. It falls onto the wooden deck, and soon the whole ship burns to a crisp.

THE END

Concrete chunks bounce off your back. No more house. No more woman.

"Move!" Celadus bellows.

He carries the baby beneath his shield. Lightning zags on Vesuvius. Was it just yesterday you gazed up at the shapely mountain outlined against blue sky?

Now it seems like a monster.

Ferox barks.

"What is it?" Spurius asks.

Ferox leads you to a girl cowering on the steps of the Temple of Jupiter. Her parents told her the god of sky and thunder would protect her. But they never came back.

Celadus passes you the baby and picks her up. Paulla.

At last you stagger into the Forum Baths. Debris covers the courtyard garden. But the walls feel strong; they survived the earthquake of '62.

Outside, Celadus hunts for more survivors. Inside, you and Spurius and Ferox hunt for the passage to the aqueduct.

Each time you check back, you find more kids sitting in marble niches. Two brothers with bloody faces. A girl with a broken arm. Paulla holds the baby. Ferox licks a toddler, who laughs.

Finally, you and Spurius locate a promising tunnel,

crouchable, with water trickling underfoot.

"We'll go first, and you bring up the rear?" you ask Celadus.

He shakes his head. "I'll follow later. With others I find."

You don't like this plan. Having Celadus around makes you feel braver. Maybe that's what it's like to have a father.

He lays one beefy hand on your shoulder and the other on Spurius. "Courage and discipline," he says. "You're gladiators now. Go."

Days later, you emerge from the waterworks in the city of Nola. It's teeming with refugees.

Vesuvius, you learn, has annihilated Herculaneum and Pompeii.

People call your group "the children of Fortuna." A tilemaker and his brother adopt all eight of you. And Ferox, of course.

They ask the babies' names. Celadus, you say. And Quinta.

THE END

"Who let him out?" Spurius asks. "I'll run him home and meet you back here."

Bad plan. But you can't ignore Ferox. Spurius can move faster alone. If anyone in town recognizes him, he's just Publius's stable boy.

"Back in a flash," he says. "Mercury isn't the only one with winged sandals."

You canvass the docks. So many different types of vessels. So much hustle and bustle.

No more barrels or amphoras rest beside the Africa ship.

Where are you, Spurius?

Moving together like the pieces of a water clock, crewmen hoist the gangplank. The ship is off.

Without you.

You have your eye on a giant corbita, still loading. Such a large merchant vessel must cross the Mediterranean.

Hurry up, Spurius.

You pace.

You okay, Spurius?

Should you go look for him? You might miss each other. He might take one street while you're heading in the other direction one block over.

You could march onto the ship now carrying one

of the pomegranate crates. But how will Spurius know you're there?

The corbita departs.

Just a few hours until daylight. Maybe Spurius fell asleep. Or changed his mind. Or Publius caught him.

Maybe you should just go back to Misenum.

You wait.

At dawn, an old fisherman struggling with ropes asks you for a hand. His no-good assistant got into a bar fight. He asks you to sail with him today, to Ischia, the big island southwest of Misenum.

It leaves your options open. You can come back for Spurius.

You're about a third of the way across the bay when Vesuvius shoots up ash.

You spend the rest of your life on Ischia. You've escaped next door.

You never learn what happened to Spurius or Pliny or Whiny. You work for the fisherman for years. He has no children. Your children call him Grandpop. When he dies, he leaves his house, boat, and nets to you.

You never read or write anything again. But you also never have to take dictation from someone in a bathtub.

THE END

With a tap of your heels, Victor continues upward. You doze, rocked by the horse. For how long? Victor hesitates. You open your eyes and cough.

Gone is the greenery of the lower slope. Blackness devours the moonlight. Smoke wisps low to the ground and around the peak. Stench thickens the air, stinging your eyes and throat. You feel woozy.

You sip from Spurius's metal canteen. Froth outlines what you can see of Victor's mouth. He needs water too. But how can you give it to him? If you get off, you might not be able to get back on. Still, it's cruel not to let him drink. You slide to the ground, hot beneath your sandals. Surely you're walking on the roof of the underworld. You splash water into your open palm and hold it out to Victor. He sucks it through his giant lips.

You can't remount.

First you grab the saddle horn, but you just can't swing up and over. Next you jump, first beside him and then with a running start. Ka-bong onto your butt.

Victor stares, wildness in his eyes. You position yourself in front of his head. "Kneel!"

He won't.

Tired, hungry, scared, you bawl. What now?

➲ **TO SEARCH FOR A WAY TO CLIMB BACK IN THE SADDLE, GO TO PAGE 82.**

➲ **TO HOWL IN FRUSTRATION, GO TO PAGE 97.**

"Ready, Sir."

Even though you're not thrilled to turn back around, this mushrooming cloud does warrant a field trip.

A messenger hurries from the waterfront with a note. Pliny's friend Rectina, who lives at the foot of Vesuvius, is begging for help.

In an instant, Pliny changes from scholar to admiral. He orders all available ships into the water—about a dozen quadriremes, with four banks of rowers each. He's leading a rescue flotilla to the Pompeii coast.

You ride with him on the *Mars*. As the oars march through the sea, the cloud spreads, veiling the sun's light. Darkness creeps down from the sky into your heart.

Pliny seems almost jolly. He dictates another chapter for *Natural History*. Since everyone is coughing—especially him—he muses about one of his favorite remedies: millipedes soaked in honey.

Waves grow wilder. Cinders and rocks plummet onto the deck. You burn your hands scrambling to throw them overboard. So many rocks have fallen into the bay that they jam the shallows.

The pilot advises Pliny to turn back.

Pliny dismisses him. "Fortune favors the brave."

But the quadrireme can't reach the shore. Or Rectina.

Pliny leaves each captain to decide his course. He directs the *Mars* south toward Stabiae.

His friend Pomponianus is pacing along the beach, which is strewn with his possessions. It's as if he's turned his villa inside out.

You've got to hand it to Pliny: He keeps his cool. Sea slamming ships onto the shore? *A little chop.* Fires on the mountainside? *Just abandoned peasant houses. Everything will blow over by morning.*

Pliny asks for a bath. Then dinner. Reluctantly, Pomponianus orders his household back into the villa.

Despite the relentless thwack of debris on the roof, Pliny eats and drinks and chats late into the evening. You settle him in bed, then lie down outside his door.

Is he sleeping? Judging by the snores, yes.

You, on the other hand, are cringing beneath the groaning roof, wondering how long until it caves in.

➲ **CONTINUE TO PAGE 84.**

You walk back to the Basilica, which always has good graffiti.

"The man I am having dinner with is a barbarian."

"Epaphra, you are bald!"

"Epaphra is not good at ball games."

"Somebody's got it in for Epaphra," you say.

"Let's eat," says Spurius.

"Bath first," I say. "Pliny's orders."

In the Forum Baths, even perfume can't quash the stench. "Don't waste your money, boys," a man says. "There's hardly any water."

You head to the carryout counter at Asellina's Tavern. "Here dwells happiness." Two marines argue by the doorpost.

"Captain's crazy to push off this evening," one says.

"He's jumpy. Wants to get our goods to Africa," his mate says.

"One drink."

You look at Spurius and roll your eyes. Yeah, right.

Back at the stable, Ferox, the mutt who is anything but ferocious, sniffs your grilled ribs. You toss him the bones.

Then you help Spurius muck out the stalls, debating.

➲ **TO RETURN TO MISENUM, GO TO PAGE 86.**

➲ **TO STAY IN POMPEII, GO TO PAGE 78.**

Spurius chooses the two best horses—the chestnut stallion and a gray one for you.

"Sarno Gate," you murmur. "If anyone asks, Publius has sent for these horses."

As you pass the amphitheater, you hear the crowd roar. It's as if they're cheering for you.

Beyond the gate, you relax under cover of darkness. After a few hours, you tie the horses to a tree and rest. Given how much Publius and his servants are probably drinking, the sun may be high before anyone notices that Spurius is gone.

At first light, you remount. This small road is unusually crowded: horses, carts, families on foot, rich men on litters carried by slaves. You and Spurius blend in.

About midday, a boom draws your attention. Thick smoke rises like a cobra from the top of Vesuvius.

Wind pushes the cloud southeast, behind you, toward Pompeii.

You ride, unsure of what is happening, where you are going, and how you will live.

Freedom is bewildering.

➲ **CONTINUE TO PAGE 77.**

Pliny dictates while he eats. You and an older scribe take turns writing on papyrus and looking up passages in books.

About an hour after sunrise, the house shakes again like a wet dog.

"Four," you say.

Pliny's sister rushes in. Plinia. She's a widow, always fussing over her son, Gaius. He's seventeen, a skinnier, wussier version of his uncle. Pliny the Younger people call him. You have a private nickname for him: Whiny Pliny.

Everyone feels sorry for Whiny since his father died young. So? Pliny helped raise him. In Rome, Whiny studied with the fanciest tutors. Not like you. You had to learn your letters by copying from books. Every time you made a mistake, someone boxed your ears.

"What's happening?" Plinia's breath is short, her voice high.

"I finished my breakfast, and I'm thinking about lunch," Pliny says.

"This shaking—"

"Has stopped."

"My maid tells me the porter told her this is just what happened before the big quake in Pompeii."

"Which quake? There are so many."

"The one that knocked down half the town. They say it happened the year I delivered my dear son."

Probably she thinks there's a connection—as if the gods

rattled out a birth announcement seventeen years ago. Never mind that Whiny was born way up north.

"Was the porter there during the quake?" Pliny asks.

"He heard people talking in the tavern."

"And drinkers in taverns are the most reliable reporters."

Just then the gods' gift to the Roman Empire joins the group. "Look at this tunic—ruined!" Whiny wails.

There's a black splot right above his belt. Bull's-eye.

"Are you all right?" his mother asks.

"I have ink all over me! Not to mention all over my poem."

"Get him a clean tunic," Plinia says to a slave. She turns to her brother. "You must send your nephew to safety. Across the bay, people have sighted giants roaming."

"Let me guess," Pliny says. "These people sighting giants had just left the tavern."

You hear tinkling just as you feel vibrations. It's as if a heavy cart is rumbling right by the villa. All the glass souvenirs from Pliny's years in Africa are dancing on the shelves. A few books slip out and slap the floor. You glance up just as a large blue-glass pitcher jigs straight to the edge—right above Whiny.

➲ **TO TRY TO DEFLECT THE PITCHER, GO TO PAGE 88.**

➲ **TO WATCH IF WHINY GETS BONKED, GO TO PAGE 48.**

You drop the torch and stamp it out. "Hide!"

Spurius slides under Lockbox I. You grab the smoldering torch, lie flat on the marble floor, and pull yourself under Lockbox II. You hope whoever's coming doesn't smell the torch.

Soft glow of a candle. Gnarly feet. Suddenly, the porter breaks into song. You wish you could cover your ears. Finally, he leaves. You worm out of your hiding spot and find another torch. The key opens Lockbox II, which contains all kinds of treasures—including the key to Lockbox I.

You place your writing tablets in a chest and stuff your pouch with what's small and unbreakable: coins, rings, necklaces. Spurius does the same. He holds up a green striped glass vase. "Take it?"

"Too big."

It slips from his hands and smashes on the floor. You both freeze. A minute passes. Two.

You lock the chests. Should you return the porter's key? Too risky. You slide it under Lockbox I, sweeping the broken glass there too with the bottom of your sandal.

Spurius whispers, "That was easy. Now—"

"What are you two doing?" the porter demands.

⮑ **TO TRY TO TALK YOUR WAY OUT OF TROUBLE, GO TO PAGE 112.**

⮑ **TO OFFER A BRIBE, GO TO PAGE 44.**

How did you find your way to this secret page? You're truly Quintus the Curious.

You're standing near the top of Vesuvius. The ground is lumpy, and haze hangs over a particularly big bump. You move a little closer.

Smoke spurts from two slashes, so close in size that they remind you of nostrils. Speaking of noses, you can't help but wrinkle yours. The whole mountainside is hot and stinky and panting. *Wait.* Mountains don't pant. Is this a geographical feature or . . . a living creature?

Before you can fully process this thought, the ground writhes beneath you. You plunk onto your butt. Black basalt softens slightly, no longer rock but rough reptilian skin covering a muscular body. Crags line up like spikes on top of a long snout—with those fuming nostrils at the end.

A dragon. And you're riding it bareback.

It twists its thick neck to face you. One snort, and you'll be a flaming marshmallow. "Hang on," it says.

You tighten the grip of your thighs and grab onto two giant scales. Behind your legs, wings pull away from the dragon's armored body. With one coordinated flap, the dragon rises in the air.

"Where to?" it asks.

You have so many questions. First, what is going on? Second, is this dragon speaking Latin, or are you suddenly fluent in Draconic? Third, how are you supposed to know where to go when you've never traveled beyond Rome and the Bay of Naples?

But if you're going to carry on a conversation, this is the most important question: "What's your name?"

"Call me Ves," the dragon says.

"Nice to meet you."

You try to remember what Pliny wrote about dragons. No venom—that's a plus. Though you still don't want Ves to bite you with those fangs. Pliny had lots of ideas about dragon parts . . . like tie the fat from a dragon's heart to your arm, and you'll win a lawsuit. But that implies you've killed the dragon, right? And why would you do that? Dragons understand the secrets of the earth. Some people even say they protect mortals. You hope they're right.

"Any suggestions, Ves? I'm kind of attached to this place."

"I recommend getting unattached for a spell. This mountain's a pressure cooker with a fire below. Ever been to China?"

"No."

"The Han dynasty's having a golden age. Art, science—pretty amazing times there. And the emperor's fond of dragons. Shall we?"

Amazing. Maybe you can write your own encyclopedia. Pliny's best chapters come from his own travels.

"Yes—but can we make a stop first?"

With just a few strokes of his giant wings, Ves flies you to Pompeii. You pick up your friend Spurius. And why not more? Ves touches down at villa after villa, young slaves running across the courtyards to climb onto the back of this magnificent beast. And then you're off—a whole dragonload of kids born with nothing soaring to great heights.

THE END

"It's not safe here," Plinia pleads. "We should return to Rome. I have only one son. Would you keep him in danger?"

"I have my work," Pliny says.

"Bring the book with you."

"What about the others?"

I glance around—shelf after shelf after shelf of books in Greek and Latin, many of them now on the floor.

"It's just papyrus," Plinia says.

Mistake. Don't tell a writer that books are nothing but woven reeds covered with ink.

"I'm admiral of the imperial fleet," Pliny reminds her. "I can't abandon my command here. What would I tell the emperor?"

"Giants," says Plinia.

"Not giants—wind. Underground wind is causing these little shakes."

Plinia refuses to let go of her giants. She's like a dog with a bone.

"What do you think, Gaius?"

"I don't know," Whiny says.

"Then I shall send you to Pompeii," Pliny says.

"Me?" Whiny squeaks.

"Rome, not Pompeii," Plinia insists. Because she's a woman, she has no say. But Pliny loves his sister.

"All right. I'll send you and Gaius to Rome, with a report for Emperor Titus. Quintus can go as your scribe."

"Not necessary," Whiny says.

"What do you think, Quintus?"

You have more thoughts than stars in the night sky.

"Sir, I think I can serve you better by going to . . . "

➲ **TO CHOOSE ROME, GO TO PAGE 11.**

➲ **TO CHOOSE POMPEII, GO TO PAGE 90.**

What would Pliny do?

Investigate, of course. But without a horse, you can't possibly hike up Mount Vesuvius and make it back in time to return to Misenum.

You finger the coins in your pouch. Forget buying or renting a horse.

Maybe you can borrow one. You ask around. You offer a coin as a token of good faith and explain that you're serving the admiral.

Everyone sidesteps you as if your humors are unbalanced.

Only one old woman responds. She's wearing a bright white tunic and a striking gold ring with a red stone.

"Here, dear," the woman says. She pulls a flask from the drawstring bag tied to her belt. "Drink this and get the demon out."

No thanks.

You could steal a horse. You quickly run through the penalties. They're steeper for slaves. Death. A lashing. Banishment to the quarries to chisel rock sixteen hours a day. Pliny wouldn't put a collar on you, would he? Or send you to gladiator school to learn how to fight to the death?

On the other hand, if you can figure out what's going on, Pliny may set you free.

You've pinched and pocketed things before. How else can slaves survive? But you've never stolen anything as big as a horse. You look around . . . and head to the public toilets.

Today the smell almost knocks you to your knees. Water isn't running well. Still, the place is teeming, as usual.

You scout the area, making a plan. While in town, men often pee into the clay jugs outside laundries. But if they need to sit, they come to the toilets. Sometimes they linger, praying or chatting. People say it's almost relaxing, with the sound of water running to push the sewage out into the street toward the bay.

Riders hitch horses to a post outside. If they have a slave, they leave their property to guard their property. Sometimes, an owner demands his slave come inside to fetch a bum cleaner.

You're looking for an unattended horse.

You spot a gray mare. She's tied next to a few stone stairs to make mounting easier.

Calmly you unhitch the mare. You fish in your pouch and give her a chestnut. Then you climb on her back and trot toward the Vesuvius Gate.

Several blocks behind you, a shout goes up. "My horse! Thief!"

You kick your heels into the mare's flank. "Go, in the name of the goddess Epona!"

You lean into her neck. As you gallop, you pray no carts will block your way. People yell from the side-walk. You rise high from the saddle, turning your head to look back over your shoulder.

Mistake.

You run SMACK into a stone arch and go flying.

Now you live with an old woman. She owns a laun-dry in some town near Rome. Your job is to empty the piss pots by the door. You mix urine with water in a large tank and wash wool with your feet. "Keep stomp-ing, dear," the woman says. "Pretend it's a demon."

If you do a good job, she lets you touch her pretty ring, gold with a red stone.

A leather pouch hangs in the kitchen. It used to con-tain papyrus with writing on it. But you and the old woman can't read, so you burned it on a cold winter day.

You have no idea who you are or why you're here, but it's not a bad life.

THE END

You fake left, then dash across the deck, leap onto the gunwale, and plunge into the sea.

You half expect Dagger-man to chase you. But then it occurs to you: He probably can't swim.

You plow through rock soup to the port. Chaos. Walls collapsing. Parents calling out for lost children. You scrabble inland and up into the city, hunched against the barrage of ash and rocks.

At last you reach Publius's back gate and pound hard. The noise is deafening.

Spurius left town?

But in the din, you hear frantic neighing and barking.

At last Spurius flings open the door. Ferox, the stable watchdog, leaps up and knocks you down.

He licks you all over the face.

"I love you too," you say.

Publius sent for his wife and children and servants after the theater. They're riding out the storm in the banker's villa.

"He left you?"

"To look after the animals. Come, come, come!"

You race into the stable. The horses stamp in their stalls.

"Friend, you smell worse than Sterculius, god of manure."

"There's skin beneath that dirt? You are uglier than Vulcan!"

What you decide next is a matter of life or death.

⊃   **TO MAKE A BREAK, GO TO PAGE 95.**

⊃   **TO SHELTER IN PLACE, GO TO PAGE 79.**

Riders of the cursus publicus thunder past with letters bound for Rome. People call out for news, but the postal messengers won't stop.

One shouts, "All is lost."

After several days, a delegation from Rome stops at an inn where you and Spurius are grabbing a rare hot meal. The emperor has appointed a board to determine how to aid survivors of the disaster. Officials need people who know the local area.

➲ **TO JOIN RELIEF EFFORTS, GO TO PAGE 87.**

➲ **TO KEEP MOVING, GO TO PAGE 30.**

The words come out before you've fully formed the thought. "We should run away."

You lay out the dangers. If you get caught, your owners could cut off your ears. Or send you to the quarries.

"I'm one bad mood away from chains anyway," Spurius says. He tugs his tunic from his shoulder for a moment, exposing scars.

Pliny's guests sometimes remark how lucky you are. It's true that your owner is no Publius. But no one is lucky to be a slave.

You lower your voices. You agree to move quickly, while Publius is at the theater. But that's about all you agree on. Spurius argues that you won't get far on chestnuts and a few coins. What will you eat? How will you travel? Where will you go?

"'Hope is the pillar that holds up the world,'" you say.

"Did you just make that up?" Spurius asks.

"Pliny."

"You're usually the one telling me to think things through."

He's right. But now you're thinking with your gut, not your head, and it's telling you to leave Pompeii fast.

➲ TO LOAD UP ON MONEY, GO TO PAGE 28.

➲ TO ESCAPE ON HORSEBACK, GO TO PAGE 61.

➲ TO HEAD TO THE PORT, GO TO PAGE 114.

With Spurius you try to bridle the horses, but they're spooked.

You know your friend. If the horses won't go, he won't either.

"Let's take them inside," you say.

"The house?"

"Why not?" You glance toward Vesuvius. You're beginning to think that nothing will matter after this. "How can that old chamber pot punish us if we save his racehorses?"

In the inner courtyard, ash has piled up so high that it covers all but the statues' eyes and hair. They stare— never seen horses clopping around inside before.

You corral the animals into the grand atrium and various bedrooms. Victor drops a big plop in Publius's office.

"That was from me," Spurius says.

You and Spurius have the run of the mansion. First, you raid the kitchen. The cook decamped in a hurry, leaving a feast half-prepared. You run around tasting— grilled boar, boiled octopus, stuffed doormouse.

Spurius finds a jug of water to mix with wine. You pile a tray with food and fruit—cherries even!—and carry it to the dining room. You dust off cushions and stretch out on the couches. Ah, this is the life.

"I'm more stuffed than that doormouse," says Spurius.

"Let's play knucklebones." Publius has an ivory set, of course—no goat knuckles for him.

With Ferox, you and Spurius roam the villa. You wish you had music to drown out the terrible sounds outside.

You decide to sleep in the room with the red silk bed-cover and tasseled pillows. Spurius lifts Ferox onto the bed. The two of you get on either side of the dog. It's hot, very hot. But the mattress is stuffed with feathers.

In the dark, you talk about your uncle Felix and his plan to buy your freedom. And once you're a freedman, you'll save to buy Spurius.

"I'm never going to obey you," he says.

One day, you'll be a lawyer, defending slaves. Spurius, the hot-shot charioteer, is going to race in the Circus Maximus in Rome in front of 20,000 spectators.

You never know what killed you.

Almost 1800 years later, an Italian archaeologist injects plaster into the ruins of Publius's villa. His casts puzzle researchers. A house full of horses? Who were these two boys, curled toward each other on either side of a dog?

THE END

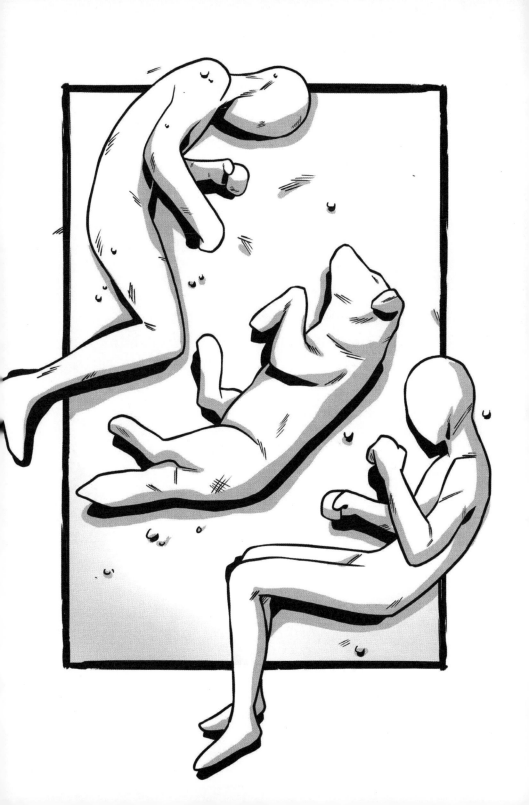

You keep climbing toward the summit. Surely you can scramble up one of the crags—they're practically ladders, right?—and leap onto Victor.

Victor huffs and tosses his head. You tug his reins. There is no path. Sharp rocks slash your shins. Everything else feels fuzzy, spinning.

Victor refuses to go on. You seem to be approaching the edge of something. A lake at the top of the mountain? You can soak your feet and fill your canteen.

You drop the reins and hurry to the rim.

Just then the ground gives way. Rockslide.

You join the stew boiling in Vesuvius's old caldera.

THE END

Crashes. Screams. You wake as slaves run through the halls. A wing of the house has buckled. Pomponianus insists everyone move outside.

Pliny doesn't want to get up. "So I can get conked on the head?"

You ask a house slave to round up belts and pillows. As family and guests gather in the atrium, you make pillow hats.

"Now I'm soft in the head," Pliny says.

You all stagger to the beach. The sea's too rough to launch any vessel. Pliny's struggling to breathe. Pomponianus orders a sail spread so Pliny can lie down.

"Water," Pliny gasps.

You get a jug and cup. Raising Pliny's head, you give him a sip. You smell sulfur.

"The air is poisoned," Pomponianus yells. His family and guests scatter.

"More water," Pliny whispers. You lift the cup again. "You've been like a son to me, Quintus."

Two of Pomponianus's slaves drag Pliny to his feet. He slumps and falls. Dead. The slaves take off. You lay Pliny back on the sail, close his eyes, and cross his hands over his chest. Then you remove his pillow hat and tie it on top of your head. Double-soft in the head.

➲ **TO STAY WITH PLINY'S BODY, GO TO PAGE 99.**

➲ **TO DISAPPEAR INTO THE NIGHT, GO TO PAGE 108.**

Morning. You skip the side trip to Herculaneum—not enough time.

"If Publius leaves, go with him," you tell Spurius.

The oarsmen look beat. You find some shade under the gunwales of the liburnian and snooze all the way back to Misenum. While sailors unload supplies, you hurry up to the villa. You find Pliny in his library.

"News, Quintus?

Before you can answer, his sister rushes in from the garden. "You must come. A cloud atop Vesuvius, like no other."

Pliny puts down his book and calls for his shoes. You follow him outside. Much of the household has gathered in the courtyard.

"Looks like an umbrella pine," he says. "With a very tall trunk and wide branches above. I must observe that cloud more closely."

Pliny sends a slave to have a light ship prepared. "Come, Gaius. Quintus, too."

Whiny has other plans, however. "I have to finish the writing you assigned me this morning, Uncle."

Quack.

"Quintus?" Pliny says.

➲ **TO PUT THE BRAKES ON THIS FIELD TRIP, GO TO PAGE 101.**

➲ **TO ACCOMPANY HIM, GO TO PAGE 58.**

You and Spurius volunteer. Emperor Titus rewards towns that welcome refugees. He decrees that any property from those who died without a will goes into a fund for survivors. He even visits Campania, twice.

You and Spurius prove indispensable to relief efforts. For a couple of years, you serve as public slaves. You set up tents, buy food, locate missing family members— whatever is needed. It feels good to do *something*.

In thanks, the government gives you and Spurius a workshop and apartment block in Rome once owned by a Pompeii wine merchant named Publius.

The emperor himself grants your freedom.

THE END

Plinia screams. You leap without thinking. You don't mean to bump Whiny so hard. (Or do you?) With him out of the way, you stretch your arms and clasp the pitcher to your chest. You're going to fall. But you position your shoulder to hit the floor first, then roll to your feet.

You shake off the pain. You saved the pitcher.

"He knocked me down," Whiny says.

"Sorry."

"Are you all right, my little duckling?" Plinia asks.

"This is just the worst day," Whiny says. *Quack.*

"Better an elbow from Quintus in the ribs than a pitcher from Alexandria on the head," Pliny says. "Amazing country, Egypt."

Oh no. He's going to launch into one of his *Natural History* lectures. First, he'll describe every bean and grain grown along the Nile. Then he'll give the dimensions of all the pyramids.

Plinia distracts him, fortunately.

➲ GO TO PAGE 68.

Your opinion doesn't matter. Pliny will do exactly as he pleases.

"Pompeii, Sir," you say. It's a hopping town.

A trip across the bay will also let you scratch the constant itch of your curiosity. Plus, you'll have a break from routine. Pliny puts every "fact" he reads or hears in his *Natural History*. About those people with sixteen toes on their feet, which face backward, how can they run when they can't see where they're going?

You can also sneak in a quick visit with Spurius. You can always count on your friend for a bit of fun.

"Good," Pliny says. "Let's not trouble the emperor until we know more."

It gets better. The admiral is sending you to Pompeii in one of the navy's liburnians, powered by twenty rowers on each side. It can raise a wide sail, too.

It gets worse. The majordomo will accompany you. The pantry needs restocking.

"Your job is to listen and to report what people are saying," Pliny says. "Bring the large tablet. Bring two."

He ticks off places to eavesdrop. "The Basilica first," he says. "When court lets out, lawyers blab. That is their talent."

Your list grows. The Forum. Municipal offices. Public baths. Amphitheater. Gladiators' barracks. Temples.

Taverns. "Just follow the oarsmen," he says.

Does he really expect you to cover this much ground?

"Where should I eat, Sir?"

"The majordomo will give you coins. And while you're in town, have a bath, Quintus. You could use one."

➲ **CONTINUE TO PAGE 14.**

A woman holding a child opens the door. She covers her mouth and gasps.

She calls into the house. At that moment the ground trembles. The woman pulls you inside just as tiles fall from the roof and smash on the step. The child cries, and she shushes him.

A man pitches from side to side in the corridor like a passenger on a boat in rough seas.

When the quake ends, you look into his face. It's almost a mirror.

"Are you my father?"

He pauses. "Uncle."

The rest of the evening passes in a blur. You hand over Pliny's letter. You tell Felix what you heard at the Forum.

"Maybe we should leave town," Felix says.

"I can't," says his wife, Julia. She's a midwife, and one of her patients is near delivery.

Felix and Julia insist you rest and share their dinner. Baby Julius sits on his mother's lap. She feeds him with her fingers.

Felix tells a story.

He grew up in Athens, under Roman rule. He studied medicine, like his father. His father had many Roman friends and joined their drinking games.

One evening, Felix's father made a mistake. The wife of an important official died.

To pay his way out of trouble, he sold Felix and his younger sister, Quinta, into slavery.

Resold and resold, Felix ended up treating soldiers in Pliny's cavalry unit.

"Pliny doesn't like doctors, especially Greek ones," you say. "He believes in natural remedies."

Felix laughs. "We had many debates."

But Felix healed many of Pliny's men. So, Pliny bought him, brought him to Rome, and set him free.

"What happened to your sister?" You can't bring yourself to say her name.

Felix hangs his head. "It took a long time, but with Pliny's help, I found her. I was saving up to free her. But she died soon after childbirth. So, Pliny bought you."

It's as if there's a belt around your heart, and someone yanked it tight. You just found your mother—and lost her again.

That night the story loops through your head. Your mother held you. She named you. You think of Julia holding Julius. You fall asleep imagining Quinta holding Quintus.

➲ **CONTINUE TO PAGE 111.**

You argue for leaving. Given what you've seen at the seaport, you'll do better on land.

Spurius disagrees. It's got nothing to do with obeying Publius. He refuses to abandon the horses.

"So, we'll ride," you say. "The first triumph of the great charioteer Spurius."

First, the two of you lash ropes together in a long line.

Next, you bridle the skittish horses, no easy task. Then, you tie the horses to the rope at intervals so they can't harass each other. You mount the first horse and grab the front of the long rope. Wading through debris, Spurius crosses the courtyard and opens the gate.

Ash immediately fills his tracks.

He plods back. From the charioteers' tack room, he brings a leather helmet for each of you. Mounting the rear horse, he picks up the end of the rope and a leash fixed to Ferox's collar.

The plan is to lead the horses through the gate, down the street, and out of town.

You can't even get them all out of the stable. Debris hammers your helmet. Horses rear and scream.

"Back," Spurius yells.

You regroup in the stable.

"We'll die here if we stay," you tell him.

You and Spurius untie the horses. They have a chance.

Unleashed, Ferox follows you and Spurius. It's a slog just to reach the street, especially for the dog, leapfrogging over debris. You pick up one of the rocks that rain from the sky. It's hard as glass yet pocked.

That would interest Pliny. If you ever see him again.

➲ **TO HEAD TO THE RIVER, GO TO PAGE 31.**

➲ **TO FIND A SAFE SPOT IN TOWN, GO TO PAGE 18.**

Pliny has taught you the ways of science. Observation. Collection of data. But what good is that in this crisis?

Only faith can save you. Now is the time for prayer. And bargaining.

You start with Mercury, god of travelers and thieves. You ask for his winged sandals to get the heck off the mountain. In return, you promise to steal whatever you can and donate it to his temple.

Nothing.

Next, you try Minerva, goddess of learning and wisdom. If she gives you safe passage back to Pliny's library, you'll work on his encyclopedia forever without complaint.

The ground is scorching your feet, and Victor's. You both dance.

You better ask Jupiter. What can you offer the top god? At the temple in Pompeii, worshippers sacrifice animals. Ox, lamb, goat . . .

You look at Victor. Horse?

You can't sacrifice your friend.

So, what can you trade?

Your own life. With all your heart, you beg Jupiter to call off this disaster. For your part, you'll beg Pliny to sign you over to the priests as a temple slave.

Immediately, the noxious gasses disappear. The earth cools. You and Victor begin the long walk back to Pompeii.

Miracles happen: You've stopped Vesuvius from erupting.

At least as a temple slave, you can probably eat a lot of grilled meat.

THE END

Ash is falling fast and thick. Like snow, which you've never seen, but Pliny described it in Chapter 61.

He loved nature. Death didn't scare him. He said people return to whatever they were before they were born.

You weren't a slave before you were born.

You think of other things Pliny said and wrote. *"True glory consists in doing what deserves to be written, in writing what deserves to be read, and in so living as to make the world happier and better for our living in it."*

You make your way back to the beached quadrireme. You join the oarsmen sheltering belowdecks.

Eventually, the horrible sounds end. You push open the hatch, through mounds of ash. A pale sun shines.

Since the ship still cannot move, you walk the beach. Whenever you meet survivors, you send them to the ship.

The next day, you direct the quadrireme to drift along the coast. You pluck people from small, leaky boats. When you spot other ships of the fleet, you command them to rescue survivors, too. They take your orders as if you really are Pliny's son.

When the sea calms, you load the admiral into the *Mars* and sail back to Misenum.

You tell Whiny about his uncle's final hours. The family reads Pliny's will. He has no children, so he adopts Whiny and leaves him everything: farms, villas, books, all the family connections.

But he didn't forget you.

I am grateful for the service of my youngest scribe. He shall go forth a free citizen of Rome with the name G. Plinius G.L. Quintus.

THE END

You're scared. No shame in the truth.

"Sir, remember you described the 'noxious and deadly vapor' when melting lead? That's the smell around Pompeii."

"Interesting," says Pliny.

"Didn't you write that 'the breathing passages should be protected'?"

"Indeed."

"I fear many will die from the gas, Sir. You shouldn't be one of them. You have unfinished work here."

Pliny's torn. You find the chapter in his encyclopedia with the passage about lead smelters. Some of them put pig bladders over their face to keep out dust and fumes.

You point out that the villa doesn't have any pig bladders handy. Or any pigs.

You convince Pliny to stay out of harm's way, more or less, in Misenum. You've saved one of the empire's greatest scholars—and yourself—from likely death. He even mentions you in one of his footnotes.

THE END

The gentle breeze and steady beat of the oars lull the majordomo and his minions. Soon they are dozing on deck. You move to the bow. You pull the black rock out of your pouch and hold it in your open palm.

The rock soaks up the sun's heat. You return it to your pouch, positioning it over the seal. Melt the wax and you've got a lot of explaining to do. But soften it, just enough . . .

Every now and then you test the seal with your thumbnail. As you hoped, it loosens, then pops off. Glancing around, you pull out the papyrus and unscroll it.

Gaius Plinius to his former slave and battlefield surgeon . . . greetings. The winds below are stirring, perhaps a forecast of some change. I send news and seek your opinion. Trust the boy. Like Mercury, he is quick and clever, though prone to thievery too. Nonetheless, your Quinta would be proud.

You read this twice, then reroll it and slip it back into the pouch. You're flattered to be compared to Mercury, the supersmart messenger god. But how does Pliny know about the trinkets you've stolen?

And who is Quinta?

You're holding the rock up to the sun again when the majordomo sidles up to you.

"An offering to Apollo? I would not have taken you as a follower of the sun god."

You tell him a warm rock soothes aches.

"Where did you learn this trick?"

"The *Natural History*." Anything you don't want to explain you can pin on Pliny.

"Let me try."

You have a bad feeling, so you dunk your hand back into your pouch. "Let me see if I've got another rock," you say. "Just for you."

Your fingers fumble for the seal. Yes!

You place it against the scroll, then press the warm rock against the wax again. It sticks!

"What have you got in there?"

"The master's papers," you say. "Very important. Private."

You ease your hand with the black rock out of the pouch. "Guess I have just this one."

The majordomo snatches it and applies it to his lower back.

"Relief?" he scoffs.

"Warm it first."

But the majordomo has reached the end of his patience, which is shorter than a toothpick. He hurls the rock into the bay.

"You may be the master's pet, and your collar may be gold," he says. "But you're still a dog."

➲ **CONTINUE TO PAGE 38.**

The cloud expands. Some people shake their heads and go back inside. But much of the town has the same idea: leave.

Felix needs to get Julia. He hands you Julius. You bounce him up and down. He's not crying, but he's not happy either.

Felix returns without his wife. She won't abandon her patient. He leaves again for the waterfront, to rent or borrow a boat. Julius whimpers, so you whistle. You razz. You make funny faces. When he laughs, you do too.

Felix bursts through the door. "Can you drive?"

You nod. Outside the day is turning into night though it is way too early for the sun to set.

The horse, Equus, is almost as old as the crummy wooden cart he pulls.

Felix loads tools and supplies and hops in the back with the baby. He directs you through the streets, jammed now. In the early darkness, voices yell. Dogs bark. You reassure Equus. Felix says it's just as chaotic by the water.

You stop at a block of wood-and-mud apartments. Felix enters and soon exits with another man supporting a very pregnant woman. Julia settles the woman in the cart. The man runs inside for a blanket. Several children peer from the door as he lays it over his wife.

Felix and Julia promise to do their best.

"Naples and then north," Felix says.

You're grateful your friend Spurius has shown you how to drive. You hope he's driving his big-shot owner, Publius, out of Pompeii right now.

You push the horse hard, but never to his breaking point. Once in a while you look over your shoulder. Felix shelters his family and the pregnant woman under a cloth he has spread over his shoulders and down his arms like the wings of a giant bird.

Vesuvius booms and crackles with lightning. Sometime after midnight, you hear a hellish roar.

Later you learn that a boiling mix of melted rock and gas barreled down the mountainside and flooded Herculaneum.

You never forget that endless night—the dark, the crush of traffic, the woman's screams. And then, at long last, a baby's cry.

Survivors stagger into Naples. Your aunt and uncle have nothing, but they treat the wounded. You help. A family of healers.

Like other refugees, your family settles. A few years later, they move to Greece, so you can study. You become a great doctor. Even Pliny would agree.

THE END

You hurry down Via dell'Abbondanza. Shoppers crowd the storefronts. Metalsmiths pound out pans. Two sailors argue in a language you don't know. Dogs bark and chicken bawk from courtyards. A carpenter notches the bottom of a table with a hammer and chisel.

Spurius's owner, Publius Lublius, has built a flashy new villa on top of ruins from the earthquake of '62. He's a wine merchant with a nasty temper and big ambitions to dominate the chariot races in Pompeii.

You pass the narrow front door on the way to the stables. Spurius works and sleeps with the horses. Which is fine by him.

He's rubbing down a chestnut racer. "What brings you crawling out of the library, Bookworm?"

"Came to find out why this town is so stinky, Dung Shoveler."

Normally, you'd trade insults for a few minutes. But Spurius is worried because the horses are antsy. The other day, Spurius was training a younger slave to drive and one of the horses bolted. Spurius yelled at the boy to cut the reins tied around his waist, but he dropped his knife. So, when the chariot fell apart, he was dragged behind the horse.

"He lives?"

"In pieces. Publius sent him to the fields, to work in chains once he can move again."

"What did Publius do to you?"

Spurius just shakes his head.

You want to cheer up your friend. But at the same time, you've got to find out what's going on with Mount Vesuvius.

➲ **TO RIDE TO THE MOUNTAIN, GO TO PAGE 21.**

➲ **TO GO DOWNTOWN WITH SPURIUS, GO TO PAGE 26.**

You scurry after Pomponianus. Outside Stabiae, you turn toward Pompeii. The fumes are so terrible that you tear a piece of cloth from your tunic and hold it over your mouth. You turn around and walk south.

A few people pass you. Their glassy eyes do not meet yours.

You walk and walk and walk. Strangers leave food by the road.

Eventually, you cross the strait to Sicilia.

Once Rome and Carthage fought here, but peace has returned to this island. You find work on farms. Thanks to *Natural History*, you impress people with your knowledge about plants and agriculture.

Eventually, you marry and buy land. It reminds you of Campania. You grow grains and grapes. As you and your family till the rich, dark soil, you marvel at the beauty of the nearby mountain, Etna.

Luckily it doesn't erupt in your lifetime.

THE END

Dead sheep? You remember the farmer in the Forum. No time to check. You chase the dawn down the mountain and into Pompeii. You're exhausted but not sleepy. So much to do.

First, you return Victor to Spurius. You tell him that he needs to go to Herculaneum.

"Yeah, Publius is just going to say, 'Salve, Spurius.'"

"Don't let him know." You pass Spurius your leather pouch with the two letters. If anyone questions him, he should pretend to be you.

"I'm Quintus, the licehead? What if someone asks me to write something?"

You pull the tablets out of the pouch and throw them over the wall.

A voice curses from the street: "Keep your stinking trash to yourself!"

Next, you hustle to the seaport. The captain's leaning against the bow of the liburnian.

"We've got to get back to Misenum," you say.

"Slaves are giving orders?"

"Sir"—now's the time to make up a whopper—"Vesuvius is about to explode."

Not all the oarsmen have reported for duty yet, so you chase them down. Barber shops. Fast-food restaurants. Asellina's Tavern. The Wolf Den.

Within an hour, the liburnian pushes off. The captain and the majordomo rag on you.

"Says the mountain's going to explode."

"The admiral will laugh."

You don't care. Within five minutes, you're sound
asleep on the deck.

➲ **CONTINUE TO PAGE 42.**

You sleep until the day's fifth hour. What a luxury! Julia has gone to tend her mother-to-be. Julius is napping.

Felix walks you through the tiny garden. He picks a fig—and wipes it on his shirt before giving it to you. Inside, he shows you his office and his tools. A drill to penetrate a skull. A scalpel to cut out a tumor. A needle to sew up torn skin.

He opens a box, full of coins.

"Your fees?"

"My savings," he says. "To buy my nephew's freedom."

"You mean—"

Boom.

You and Felix hurry outside. People are pouring into the street, bubbling with questions. "Vesuvius," someone shouts.

Felix runs into the house for Julius, then together you jog to a spot with a view. A gigantic, murky plume unfurls above Mount Vesuvius.

"I must get back to the ship in Pompeii," you say.

"Stay with us," Felix says. "We'll send Pliny a message."

➲ **TO STICK WITH FELIX, GO TO PAGE 104.**

➲ **TO RETURN TO POMPEII, GO TO PAGE 35.**

"Bringing the mistress her jewelry," you say. "She wants to wear something special to the theater."

"Who is this?" the porter demands.

"The admiral's messenger," Spurius says.

You dig out Pliny's letter. The porter can't read, but it looks official.

"Pliny the Elder is part of the theater party," you say. "Representing the emperor."

"That's why she needs to dress to impress," Spurius says.

The porter looks doubtful. "Where'd you get the key?

"I took it from your room," Spurius says. "Didn't want to wake you."

You bend down and pull the key out from under the lockbox. "He's always dropping things," you say. "Here, Sir. We'll tell Publius you were most helpful."

The porter leaves, harumphing.

➲ **GO TO PAGE 61.**

"Remember those marines outside the tavern?" you ask.

"Going to Africa?"

"Maybe they could carry a little extra cargo."

You and Spurius strategize about stowing away. If you hide until the ship's underway, it won't matter if the crew discovers you. The captain can put you to work. Or drop you at the next port.

"Or toss us overboard," Spurius says.

You decide to leave everything behind. If a slave-hunter captures you, nothing will tie you to Pliny or Publius.

Everything. Even Ferox.

You scratch the dog's ears. Spurius sits in the hay and gives Ferox a full-on hug.

You slip out the back gate. Ferox howls.

"Shhh," Spurius says through the wall. He swipes his arm across his eyes.

As usual after dusk, torches light storefronts. You stick to the shadows, out the Marina Gate, down to the port.

It's busier than usual for this late hour. Traders argue with captains over prices. Stevedores unload huge terracotta amphoras from carts and haul them up gangways.

The earth shakes. For a moment, all activity halts as people plant their feet. Pottery smashes, followed by the pungent smell of garum, the fish sauce sent round the empire. Objects splash into water. Curses follow.

As soon as the ground stills, work resumes—with even more urgency.

You and Spurius find the Africa-bound ship. As you're scheming about how to get on board, you hear a familiar bark along the waterfront.

Ferox.

➲ **TO DEAL WITH FEROX, GO TO PAGE 55**

➲ **TO HIDE FROM FEROX, GO TO PAGE 33.**

THE TRUE EVENTS
BEHIND POMPEII

POMPEII: A BRIEF TIMELINE

New information and new interpretations change how we understand history. Until recently, most sources said that ash and molten rock buried Pompeii in August 79. Years later, Pliny the Younger wrote an eyewitness letter describing the eruption. Although that letter disappeared, a translation by a medieval monk survived—with the August date. But copyists often made mistakes.

Recent archaeological finds suggest that Vesuvius erupted in autumn. One piece of evidence: graffiti dated the middle of October 79 about someone eating too much! Other clues include the fallout of ash and rock. The pattern makes more sense with the usual fall/winter winds. Also, many victims were wearing heavy clothes. Houses had small coal heaters. And fall fruits filled pantries: dried figs, walnuts, chestnuts, and pomegranates (source: *Earth-Science Reviews*, Volume 231, 2022). As Pliny the Elder once wrote: "The only certainty is that nothing is certain."

Here's a best-estimate timeline:

700 BCE | SETTLEMENT: *Oscans build a village at the mouth of the Sarno River on a hill above the Bay of Naples. Etruscans, Samnites, and a nearby Greek colony influence the regional culture.*

200 BCE | TRADE: *Pompeii lies 14 miles (23 km) southeast of Naples and 6 miles (10 km) from Mount Vesuvius. Its location, connected to the Mediterranean Sea, makes it an ideal crossroads for trade. Pompeians form an alliance with Rome. This gives them access to overseas markets.*

90-88 BCE REBELLION: *City-states like Pompeii revolt against Roman rule in the Social Wars. They want full citizenship.*

80 BCE COLONIZATION: *Roman general Lucius Cornelius Sulla conquers Pompeii, which becomes a Roman colony.*

80-70 BCE | BUILDING: *Two prominent Pompeians underwrite an amphitheater, one of the oldest built of stone.*

73-71 BCE | UPRISING: *Spartacus, an enslaved gladiator, escapes and hides out on Mount Vesuvius. There he organizes an army of escaped slaves. They take on the Romans, win some battles, but ultimately get defeated.*

TURN OF THE 1ST CENTURY (27 BCE-14 CE)—POMPEII BECOMES A PLAYGROUND: *Rome citizens integrate with the local elite. The city prospers.*

62 CE | A BIG EARTHQUAKE: *An earthquake damages Pompeii, Herculaneum, and a few other towns in Campania. A few locals move away, but most begin rebuilding. The gladiator barracks become a private home.*

64 CE | A SMALLER EARTHQUAKE: *One historian reports that the Emperor Nero was in Naples at the time performing; he sang through the quake.*

79 CE | ERUPTION:

— *Titus succeeds his father, Vespasian, as Roman emperor. Mount Vesuvius erupts, burying Pompeii, Herculaneum, and the surrounding towns under ash and debris.*

— **FOUR DAYS BEFORE:** *Tremors and water problems that have bedeviled the region intensify.*

DAY 1 (PERHAPS OCTOBER 24)

- *Noon: Ash falls, spreading east/southeast from Vesuvius.*

- *1pm: A column of ash and volcanic rock blasts high into the air. Pliny the Elder and Pliny the Younger witness this from afar in Misenum.*

- *Afternoon and evening: Many residents of the Pompeii region flee. Pliny the Elder sets out with a dozen ships to rescue friends and survivors.*

- *Debris piles up in Pompeii and Stabiae, and the weight of it collapses roofs. Many people run to the beach.*

- *Pliny the Elder's helmsman advises him to turn back.*

- *He lands at Stabiae, about 2.8 miles (4.5 km) from Pompeii.*

DAY 2

- *1 am: The first pyroclastic surge—a superheated river of ash, gas, and liquid rock—speeds down the western slope of Vesuvius. It, and a subsequent surge, destroys Herculaneum.*

- *6:30-7:30 am: Two more surges finish off Pompeii.*

- *Pliny the Elder dies near Stabiae.*

- *Two final surges cover the countryside.*

AFTERMATH: *Emperor Titus organizes relief aid for survivors and visits Campania.*

80 CE | ROME BURNS (AGAIN): *Emperor Titus visits*

Campania again. While he's away from Rome, a big fire burns for three days.

1631 CE | A DEADLY ERUPTION: *A days-long eruption that begins on December 16 triggers a tsunami in the Bay of Naples and buries villages under pyroclastic surges. Vesuvius has erupted multiple times over the centuries, but this event has the highest death toll: about 4,000 people.*

1738 CE | DISCOVERING HERCULANEUM: *Exploring on behalf of the king, Spanish military engineer Rocque Joaquin de Alcubierre digs into Herculaneum, though he doesn't realize this at first.*

1748 CE | UNCOVERING POMPEII: *A cave-in near an area called La Cività draws Alcubierre and his excavation crew. Later they realize they've stumbled onto the ruins of Pompeii.*

1863–75 CE | GIVING FORM TO THE DEAD: *Italian archaeologist Giuseppe Fiorelli improves excavation practices and develops a technique for making plaster casts that capture the last moments of Pompeii's residents.*

1943 CE | CASUALTY OF WAR: *American and British bombers targeting German forces during World War II damage the Pompeii ruins.*

1997 CE | WORLD TREASURE: *The United Nations Educational, Scientific and Cultural Organization (UNESCO) declares the Archaeological Areas of Pompei, Herculaneum, and Torre Annunziata a World Heritage Site.*

2013 CE | REINVESTING: *The Italian government and the European Commission launch The Great Pompeii Project to reverse the deterioration of Pompeii's archaeological sites.*

Sylvia Whitman

THE TWO PLINYS

Pliny the Elder and Pliny the Younger were real people.
Pliny the Elder had a distinguished career and was
serving as the admiral at the naval base in Misenum when
Vesuvius erupted. He was a polymath, a learner interested
in many subjects. He wrote about everything from grammar
to history to lance throwing, but almost all of his work has
been lost except *Natural History*.

This encyclopedia includes a glowing description of
Campania, with its "plains so fertile, hills so sunny, glades
so safe, woods so rich in shade." It also captures Pliny the
Elder's wit and wisdom. Some of his famous quotes include
"There is no book so bad it does not contain something
good" and "Home is where the heart is."

Pliny the Elder had no wife or children, so he took under
his wing Pliny the Younger, his sister's son. Pliny the
Younger became a lawyer at age 18 and served the empire as
a high-ranking administrator. On the side, he wrote poems
and speeches and many letters, some of which he published.

The historian Tacitus asked Pliny the Younger for his
memory of the Pompeii disaster. Written 25 years after the
eruption, Pliny the Younger's letter to Tacitus is the only
surviving eyewitness account of the eruption and of his
uncle's death.

Thanks to his vivid description, volcanologists now
speak of "Plinian eruptions"—when stratovolcanoes
violently explode and shoot plumes of ash miles into the air.

BOOM! THE SCIENCE OF POMPEII

Earth has a fiery core. Gasses and melted rock, known as magma, rise because they're hotter and lighter than their surroundings. Water boils, expanding into steam. All this presses up against the planet's crust.

Earth's surface isn't a smooth sheet of rock covered by land and ocean. Rather it's a rough jigsaw of extremely slow-moving plates. Earthquakes and volcanoes most often occur in the chinks where these tectonic plates bump, rub, or split. After seismic events, the area may quiet down, temporarily (becoming dormant) or forever (becoming extinct).

Considered a "relatively young" volcano, Vesuvius formed less than 20,000 years ago as the African Plate pushed under the Eurasian Plate. It's a stratovolcano, shaped like a cone, with a bowl-shaped crater called a "caldera." When magma hits the surface, it cools rapidly into lava. Thick, sticky lava doesn't flow far, building steep sides around the vent. (Thin, runny lava creates the gentle slopes of shield volcanoes.) Each eruption added new layers to Vesuvius.

No one knows why Vesuvius woke up in 79 AD after hundreds of years sleeping. A strong earthquake in 62 destroyed buildings in Pompeii and Herculaneum—perhaps warning of the pressure building up below the surface. The many tremors in the four days before the 79 eruption also signaled stress. But Romans didn't understand plate tectonics. They didn't even have a word for volcano.

In 79, Vesuvius experienced the two most explosive types

of volcanic eruptions—Plinian and Pelean. In the initial Plinian eruption, gasses trapped in thick magma blew out, pulverizing rock into fragments. These ranged in size from grit to pebbles to bombs and blocks. All that shot up the vent through the crater. Like a rocket blasting off, the cloud traveled miles into the sky.

This phase lasted perhaps 18 hours, with ash first (rock dust, glass, minerals), then a dark cloud full of gas and debris. The wind carried this southeast, sparing Herculaneum. The air likely smelled of rotten eggs (hydrogen sulfide) and struck matches (sulfur dioxide). Static electricity touched off lightning strikes.

A blizzard of solids snowed under Pompeii. Hot ash and bits of lava, limestone, and pumice fell at a rate of about 6 inches (15 centimeters) per hour. They heated roof tiles and ignited fires. Buildings collapsed under the weight. Pumice—liquid rock cooled so fast that it's porous—landed in the bay and the river and floated.

As gasses expanded, they could no longer hold all that debris. The towering cloud began to collapse in on itself.

About 13 hours after the cloud appeared, the volcano ejected the first of six pyroclastic surges, part of a Pelean eruption. Plinian debris soars high in the sky; Pelean debris sticks low to the ground. These surges ranged from several hundred to more than 450 degrees F (232 degrees C). These superheated slurries of gas, dust, ash, and rocks roared down the side of Vesuvius, roasting everything in their path.

Traveling as fast as a car on a highway (about 67 miles per hour/30 meters per second), two pyroclastic surges incinerated

Herculaneum, including 300 people in a boathouse along the bay, perhaps awaiting rescue. "Mercifully death was quick as their brains quickly boiled and their skulls exploded," one expert put it.

Vesuvius alternated between Plinian and Pelean eruptions. A third pyroclastic surge reached the walls of Pompeii, and a fourth rolled over the city. Two more covered the countryside.

The terror lasted about 30 hours. Scholars estimate about 10 percent of the population of Herculaneum and Pompeii died, more than 2,000 people.

Vesuvius has erupted multiple times since it buried Pompeii. But people continue to live in the area. Volcanic ash and rock contain minerals such as iron, calcium, and phosphorous. When they erode, they create rich, fertile soil. And geothermal activity creates delightfully warm mineral springs.

DAILY LIFE IN THE 1ST CENTURY

Vesuvius turned Pompeii into a time capsule. The ash and lava froze a moment in daily life, giving the modern world a glimpse of the ancient one.

BATHS

Romans considered themselves better than other people. One sign of their superiority? A daily bath. They took pride in cleanliness and otium, leisure time to improve mind and body.

The Roman workday ended in mid-afternoon, when most

people headed to the public baths. Forget tiny tubs. Think fancy gyms or spas. Bath complexes included changing rooms, outside exercise areas, swimming pools, cold rooms, hot rooms, snack bars, and attendants who could give massages or pluck out hair. People often carried hand-held scrapers called "strigils" to remove dirt, oil, and sweat before a bath. Some baths had separate facilities for men and women. Others set aside separate times.

Grand villas often had private baths or swimming pools. But Romans rich and poor, free and enslaved, enjoyed the busy, noisy public baths. There they heard the latest news and gossip before heading home for dinner.

GRAFFITI

People drew and wrote all over the walls in Pompeii in Latin. Archaeologists have found political ads, crude boasts, and messages between friends. *Priscus, the engraver, to Campanus, the gem-maker: wishing you well!*

So, what does that tell us about who could read or write?

Probably only rich children attended school. One painting shows students at the Forum with tablets on their knees while a man spanks a boy with a lash. But found documents—such as a business agreement between two women—and graffiti around town suggest that a range of Pompeians had an informal education—at least enough to post rewards and menus and love letters. Said one tagger: *I'm amazed, oh wall, that you haven't fallen into ruins since you hold the boring scribbles of so many writers.*

SLAVES

Enslaved people made up 10–20 percent of the population of the Roman Empire. In Rome and throughout Italy, the concentration was higher. Many were foreigners, often war captives. But abandoned babies and homegrown Romans ended up slaves as well. Anyone born to a slave became a slave.

Since slavery wasn't race based, slaves looked no different from other members of Roman society. The Senate considered requiring special slave clothes instead of regular tunics but nixed that idea. If slaves could identify each other—and realize their numbers—they might rebel.

Slave roles ranged from baker to executioner and every job in between. Fictional Quintus is a literati, a reader and a writer. Many slaves fought as gladiators, combating wild animals or fierce opponents. If gladiators survived, they could sometimes trade on their celebrity for freedom.

The treatment of slaves depended on the whims of owners. Stories of terrible cruelty circulated: One owner fed a slave who made a mistake to man-eating eels. Farm-working slaves suffered on chain gangs. Pliny the Elder owned several estates and 4,000 agricultural slaves, but he boasted that he didn't chain them.

At the same time, Rome recognized formal and informal manumission, the granting of freedom. Some owners gave it; others let slaves buy it. With formal (legal) manumission, male slaves became Roman citizens in every way except the right to hold office. (Their children could, however.) But some freedmen could never escape the stigma of slavery.

In December, the weeklong celebration of Saturnalia turned roles and customs upside down. Everyone wore comfy clothes and took a break. Slaves could gamble and drink; they ate with their owners as equals and had the right to speak freely. To a point. They knew that after this wild holiday, their owners might hold a grudge.

A FEW FACTS THAT MIGHT SURPRISE YOU:

- Pompeii produced the wildly popular (and nutritious) fish-gut paste called "garum." Think of it as the ancient Roman equivalent of ketchup or soy sauce.

- Pompeians didn't eat spaghetti with tomato sauce. Noodles, probably invented in Asia, hadn't reached the Mediterranean yet. And tomatoes didn't appear until Europeans brought them back from the New World during the age of exploration.

- Gladiators gorged on beans, wheat, and barley. In fact, their nickname was "barley boys." Carbs helped them bulk up, and layers of fat and muscle helped protect them from fatal stab wounds.

- Roman men, women, and children—enslaved or free— drank mostly wine mixed with water and spices.

- Rome had a urine tax. Wealthy businessmen in the 1st century paid for urine collected in cesspools and public toilets. Pee contains ammonia, useful in tanning animal hides into leather and bleaching white fabric, particularly wool.

ABOUT THE CREATORS

SYLVIA WHITMAN, a writer and educator, has published a slew of articles and more than a dozen fiction and non-fiction books for young readers, including the middle-grade novel *If You Meet the Devil, Don't Shake Hands*. She lives in Sarasota, Florida, with Zulu, her porky shorkie. Find her at www.sylviawhitmanbooks.com.

MIKE ANDERSON is a comic book artist, illustrator, and animator. A proud husband, father, and year-long Halloweener, Mike loves pizza in an indecent manner. His clients include Scholastic, Subway, and Walmart, among others.

MILK & COOKIES is the middle-grade imprint of Bushel & Peck Books, a children's publisher with a special mission. Through our Book-for-Book Promise™, we donate one book to kids in need for every book we sell. Our beautiful books are given to kids through schools, libraries, local neighborhoods, shelters, and nonprofits, and also to many selfless organizations that are working hard to make a difference. So thank you for purchasing this book! Because of you, another book will make its way into the hands of a child who needs it most. Do you know a school, a library, or an organization that could use some free books for their kids? We'd love to help! Please fill out the nomination form on our website, and we'll do everything we can to make something happen.